BEAR WEATHER

By Lillie D. Chaffin

Pictures by Helga Aichinger

The Macmillan Company
Collier-Macmillan Limited, London

The Macmillan Company
Collier-Macmillan Canada, Ltd., Toronto, Ontario

Library of Congress catalog card number: 69-10498

Printed in the United States of America
First Printing

For Tom and Tommy

U. S. 1490469

Streams froze solid; ground did, too.

Bare trees shook in the wind that blew.

Snowflakes fluttered and danced and fell.

Folks all said, ''A long cold spell.''

But the big brown bear

And the small brown bear

Just didn't care.

They didn't care at all, at all;
They didn't care at all.

Snug and warm in their deep, dark den,

Cuddled up close with cheek to chin,

Sleeping through dark, sleeping through light,

They never knew the day from night.

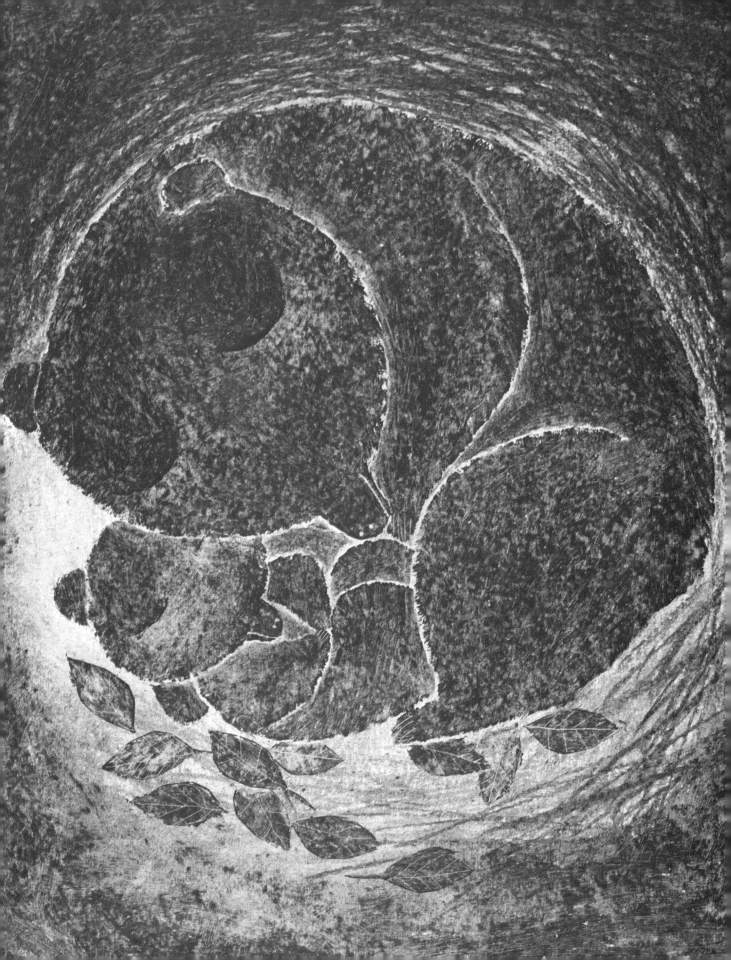

Windows were shuttered; fires grew brighter.

Folks all shivered, wrapped clothes tighter.

Barometer dropped; temperature too.

Folks all said, "What can we do?"

But the big brown bear

And the small brown bear

Just didn't care.

They didn't care at all, at all;

They didn't care at all.

Huddled up close with cheek to chin,

They opened their mouths, let the flakes drop in.

They stretched a bit, gave a yawn,

Never saw twilight, noon, or dawn.

Barometer climbed; temperature rose.

Folks shed some of their winter clothes.

Rain came down, and up came mud.

Folks all said, "A midwinter flood."

But the big brown bear

And the small brown bear

Just didn't care.

They didn't care at all, at all;

They didn't care at all.

Close and warm in their deep, dark den,

They snuggled farther and farther in.

Their bed was leaves; their world was high;

Their world was soft and fair and dry.

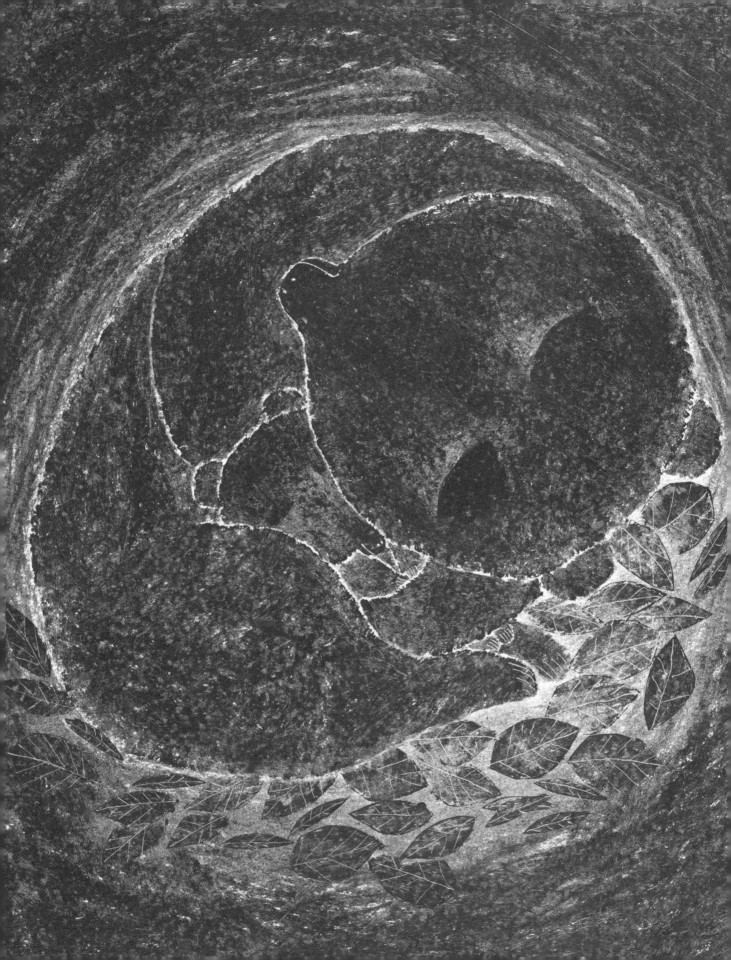

Snow blew left and snow blew right.

Snow blew around and around all night.

Before the fire, forgetting chores,

Folks all said, ''A blizzard outdoors.''

But the big brown bear

And the small brown bear

Just didn't care.

They didn't care at all, at all;

They didn't care at all.

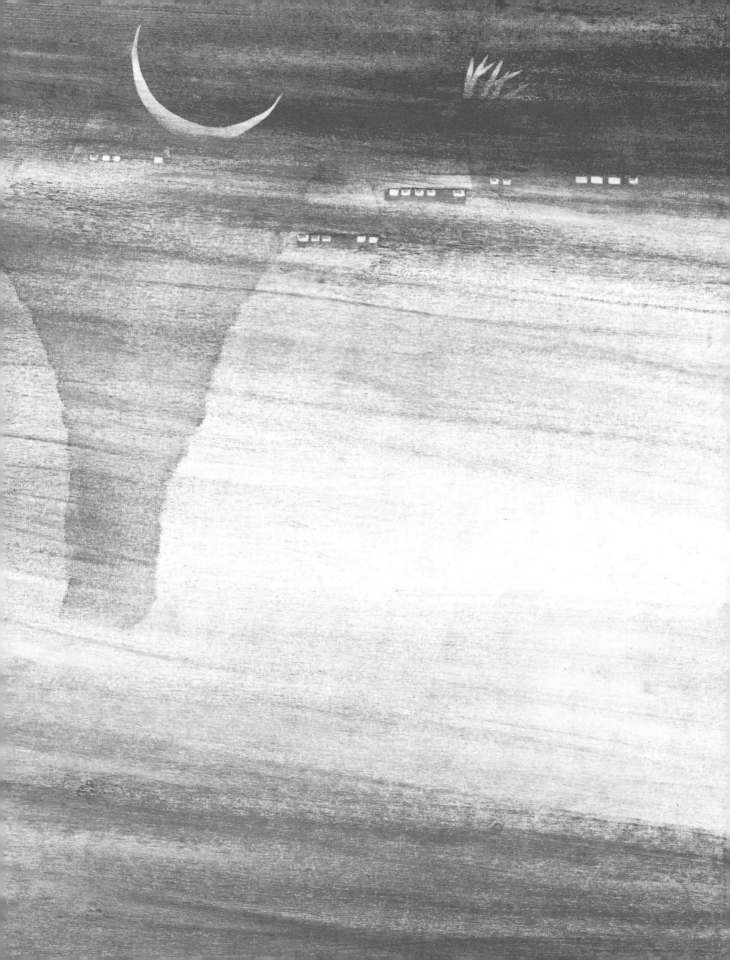

Snowflakes melted; ground peeped through.

Streams started running; south wind blew.

Leaf buds swelled; grass sprang up.

Tulips caught sun in their petal cups.

The two brown bears, in their stuffy den,

Yawned and stretched and yawned again.

Some folks said, ''We'll miss the snow.

Where, oh where, did the winter go?''

But the big brown bear

And the small brown bear

Just didn't care.

They didn't care at all, at all;

They didn't care at all.

The big brown bear rolled over, and then

Wiggled her nose, lifted her chin,

Sat up, patted the small brown bear,

And brushed a dry leaf from his hair.

"It's time to get up,"

She said, "and see

If the world is water

And a honey tree."

The big brown bear took a step, then two.

The small bear stopped, for a better view;

He wobbled a little, to and fro,

Behind his mother, and said, "Let's go."

Two steps, four steps—they stood outside,

In a world so tall and bright and wide;

They lifted their heads, stood on their toes.

The small brown bear twitched his nose.

He said, "What's this and that? Oh, look!"

"This," said his mother, "is a brook,

And that, I think, is a honey tree.

Let's take a sip, a taste, and see."

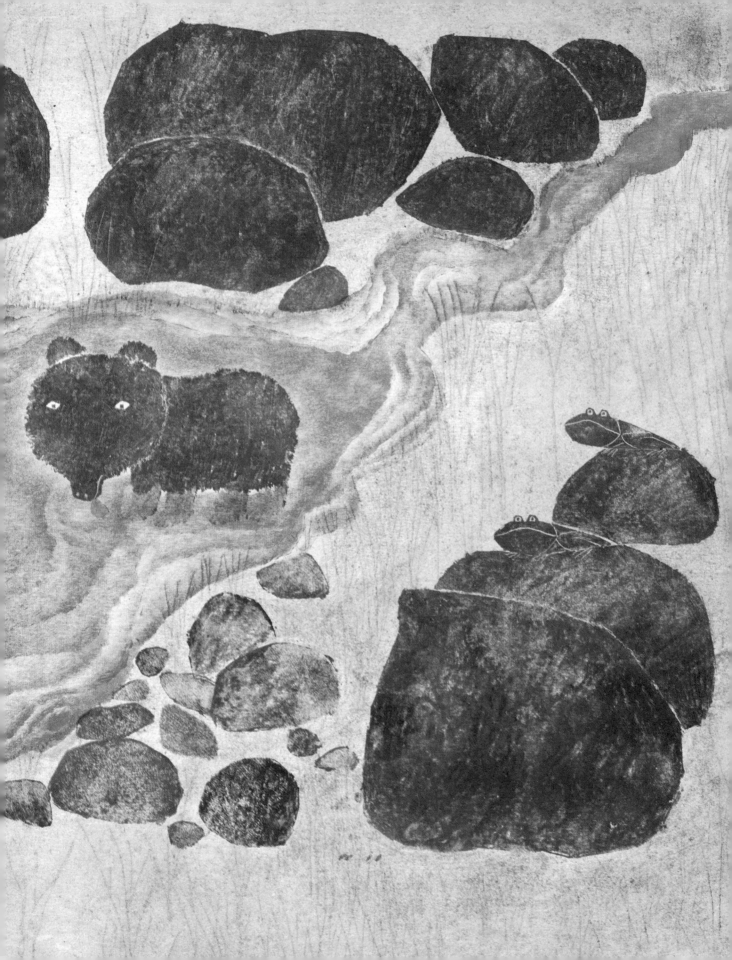

And while they tasted, a bat flew in,

To make his home in their deep, dark den.

But the big brown bear

And the small brown bear

Just didn't care.

They didn't care at all, at all;

They didn't care at all.